This book belongs to

Orlagh

This edition published by Parragon Books Ltd in 2014

Parragon Books Ltd
Chartist House
15–17 Trim Street
Bath BA1 1HA, UK
www.parragon.com

ISBN 978-1-4723-8186-6

Printed in China

DISNEY MOVIE COLLECTION
A SPECIAL DISNEY STORYBOOK SERIES

TINKER BELL AND THE
PIRATE
FAIRY

PaRRagon

Bath · New York · Cologne · Melbourne · Delhi
Hong Kong · Shenzhen · Singapore · Amsterdam

It was another busy day for the fairies of Pixie Hollow. A fairy named Zarina was strolling towards the Pixie Dust Depot where she worked. As fairies use pixie dust to fly, the other fairies assumed Zarina was walking because she had run out of pixie dust, which was surprising, since she was a dust-keeper fairy!

All of Pixie Hollow relied on the pixie dust that Zarina packaged at the Depot. She was completely fascinated by pixie dust. She had just sprinkled some on her hair to see what it would do, when the head dust-keeper, Fairy Gary, appeared. Today, it was Zarina's turn for Blue Dust Duty.

As Zarina followed Fairy Gary to the Blue Pixie Dust vault, she peppered him with questions. She wanted to know if they could make other colours of pixie dust.

Fairy Gary warned her, "Dust-keepers are forbidden to tamper with pixie dust." As she transferred some of it to a small bottle, Gary also reminded her that she was not allowed to touch the Blue Dust directly.

When the bottle was ready, Zarina and Fairy Gary flew up to the boughs of the Pixie Dust Tree. Fairy Gary poured the Blue Dust into the special container at the top. Instantly, the amount of golden dust the tree produced flowed faster and grew brighter.

"Takes the golden dust from a trickle to a roar," Fairy Gary explained.

Later, back at her cottage where she had been
secretly saving up her pixie dust, Zarina found a speck
of Blue Dust in her hair. She was inspired to try again
one of her many failed pixie-dust experiments, this time
adding a tiny bit of the Blue Dust. Suddenly, the dust
turned orange and a smile lit up her face.

Zarina couldn't wait to show Tinker Bell her discovery. She brought Tink to her cottage and showed her how the orange dust let her bend moonbeams.

"I'm doing more!" declared Zarina. And she put Tink to work stirring while various pots of dust began to explode around them. Soon they had purple dust that let Zarina create a fast-flying whirlwind.

To make pink dust, Zarina had used two slivers of the Blue Dust.

"Zarina, I really think you should stop!" Tink said firmly.

Surprised by Tink's reaction, Zarina bumped into a table and spilled all of the pink dust onto a nearby plant.

Suddenly, thick vines sprouted from the plant and tore through the cottage.

The vines twisted and turned, spreading across Pixie Hollow and destroying everything in their path – including the Dust Depot!

Queen Clarion wanted to know what had happened, and as soon as
Fairy Gary saw the pink dust, he knew it was Zarina. She tried to apologize,
but he interrupted to tell her she could no longer be a dust-keeper.

Zarina was devastated. She rushed back home, packed her things
and left Pixie Hollow.

A year passed without a word from Zarina
and it was time for the annual Four Seasons Festival.
   All the fairies gathered at the amphitheatre to see
a show that displayed talents from every season.
   Tink watched from backstage as the winter fairies
displayed their ice-skating skills.

"That's my sister!" said Tink proudly as
Periwinkle frosted flowers in front of the crowd.
She then went back to work on an elaborate
music box for her part of the show.

While everyone was watching the show, Tink and her friends spotted Zarina emerging from the shadows. She sprinkled pink dust behind the crowd. Soon, big, red poppies began to sprout around the amphitheatre.

Rosetta knew the pollen from the flowers would put everyone to sleep. "Guys! We gotta hide! Now!" she cried.

As the fairies hid backstage, Zarina flew to the dust vault.

Clank had missed the beginning of the show, so when he arrived at the amphitheatre, he was shocked to find that every last fairy was asleep. Then he heard cries for help from backstage. Tink and her pals were trapped inside the music box!

After Clank had freed them, the fairies looked at the snoozing audience. The fairies didn't understand why Zarina had put everyone to sleep. Then Clank spoke up. "I saw her flying towards the Dust Depot!"

When they got to the Depot, Zarina was gone –
and so was the Blue Pixie Dust! Zarina had taken it.
"Why would Zarina do this?" asked Vidia.
The fairies knew they had no choice but to find Zarina.
Their supply of golden pixie dust depended on that Blue Dust!
Tink asked Clank to take care of all the sleeping fairies,
then set off with her friends to find Zarina before it was too late for
Pixie Hollow!

The fairies zoomed through the woods after Zarina.

As they struggled to catch up, a heavy fog rolled in. Silvermist explained that they were nearing the coast.

The fairies flew higher and spotted a pirate ship off in the distance!

"They must have captured her and forced her to take the dust," said Tink.

Sure enough, a small rowing boat carrying three
pirates was making its way towards the ship.
The fairies looked in and saw a blue glow!

Inside the boat, Zarina was holding up the Blue Pixie Dust triumphantly.

"Let me just say your plan worked perfectly ... Captain," said James, the cabin boy.

The other pirates, Port and Starboard, bowed to their tiny leader.

The fairies couldn't believe it – Zarina was now a pirate!

"Let's just get the dust and get out of here," said Tink.

The fairies sprang into action. Rosetta grew seaweed that held the oars in place. Iridessa reflected a moonbeam into James's eyes, making it hard for him to see. Silvermist rocked the boat with a wave. Finally, Vidia snatched the Blue Dust and tossed it to Tink.

The fairies headed for the shore, but Zarina soon caught up with them and demanded that they return the dust.

Tink refused. "This dust belongs to Pixie Hollow," she said.

Zarina reached into her pocket and threw a fistful of multicoloured pixie dust at the fairies.

The dust pushed Tink and her friends backward through a waterfall. Zarina grabbed the bag of Blue Dust and quickly flew away.

Zarina's strange dust had knocked the fairies out. When Tink and the others woke up, they discovered that the colourful dust had switched their talents and outfits!

Tink was now a water fairy! She tried to part a nearby waterfall so she could pass through, but Silvermist, now a fast-flying fairy, bumped Tink as she passed by. Tink lost control over the water, which then pushed the fairies down a long, winding leaf.

The friends rode the leaf down to a beach, where Rosetta landed on a crocodile egg. The egg started to crack and a baby croc hatched from it. He hugged Rosetta tightly. Rosetta was startled – she wasn't used to her new animal talent!

"It's okay! They become attached to the first thing they see," Fawn reassured her.

Tinker Bell suddenly noticed that the pirate ship
was gone. The fairies could not fly because their wings
were wet so Vidia, who was now a tinker fairy, took
charge. She made a boat out of the croc egg. The fairies
climbed in and fast-flying Silvermist pulled them along
the water.

Then a giant wave carried them straight to the ship,
and into one of the cannons!

"Twenty-one gun salute
to the captain!" announced
a pirate named Yang.

"Out, out, out!" Tink ordered her friends. The fairies escaped just in time and saw the pirates toasting Zarina. She had promised to make the pirates fly!

The pirate crew couldn't wait.
They imagined travelling the skies beyond
the second star, dropping down on the
Mainland wherever they pleased. It was
going to be so easy to steal lots of treasure.
After all, no one would be able to catch a
pirate that flew!

Tink and the other fairies flew up to the crow's nest. Suddenly, they were gripped by fear. The pirate ship was sailing straight for the dreaded Skull Rock. That dark and scary cave was the last place they wanted to go!

When the ship passed through the rock's open mouth, the fairies were shocked to see a Pixie Dust Tree inside the cave.

"Zarina must have grown it!" exclaimed Silvermist.

"So that's how they're going to fly. She's going to make pixie dust!" Tink concluded.

The ship docked inside the cave. Zarina went to her cabin where James had brought her some food. Tink, Vidia and Silvermist slipped in behind him, while the others listened through the door.

James watched Zarina preparing the Blue Pixie Dust. "So the secret is to put the Blue Dust directly into the tree. Very impressive, Captain!" he said.

Zarina jingled as she poured the Blue Dust into a bottle. Because James was the only pirate who could understand fairy language, he had become her most trusted friend.

The fairies joined back up with Rosetta,
Iridessa and Fawn and quickly followed Zarina
to the Pixie Dust Tree. Unfortunately,
Iridessa – now a garden fairy –
accidentally touched a branch,
which made it grow so
violently that it pushed
them out of their hiding
place and straight
into Zarina!

Zarina whistled and the pirates arrived. They captured
Tink and the other fairies in a net.

"Don't do this," pleaded Tinker Bell. "Come back home.
You don't belong here."

Zarina refused. "This is exactly where I belong," she declared.

"We appreciate what she can do," James chimed in.
"Treasure it, actually."

Zarina ordered the ship's cook
to take the fairies away. He put
them in a crab cage in his galley
and locked it tight.

"Welcome to your new cabin,"
he said.

Meanwhile, Zarina added Blue Pixie Dust to the Pixie Dust Tree. Everyone held their breath and waited. The tree glowed and shook, and then ... produced a tiny bit of golden pixie dust!

"We're going to fly!" James cried. Zarina beamed at him with happiness.

In the galley of the ship, Tink and her friends had
lifted their crab-cage prison off the ground and stuck
their legs between the slats so they could run away.

But the cook stopped them from escaping by putting the crate on a table and weighing it down with a sack of potatoes.

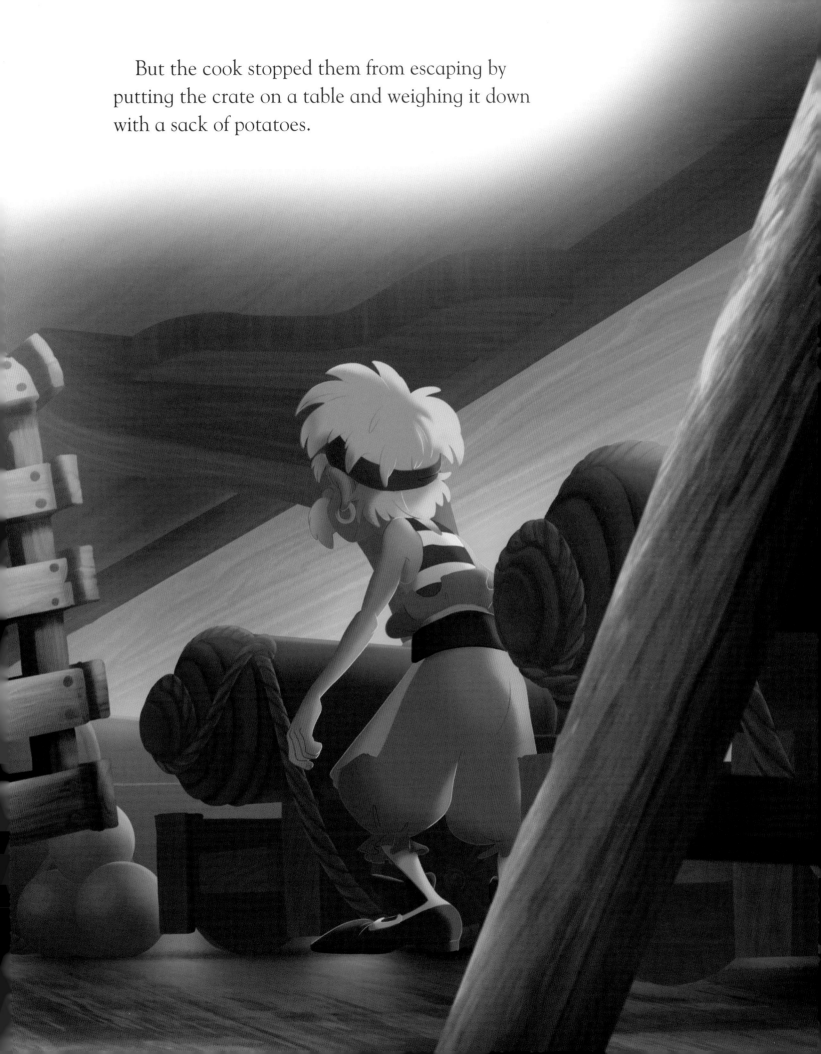

Meanwhile, the pirates were celebrating outside at the Pixie Dust Tree. The golden pixie dust was flowing steadily from it!

Zarina sprinkled some on James and taught him how to fly.

"As long as we have the Blue Dust, we'll never run out of pixie dust, right Zarina?" he asked.

"Yes," Zarina jingled back.

"Well, then, we won't need you anymore," James
announced! He grabbed the stunned Zarina and locked her
inside a lantern!

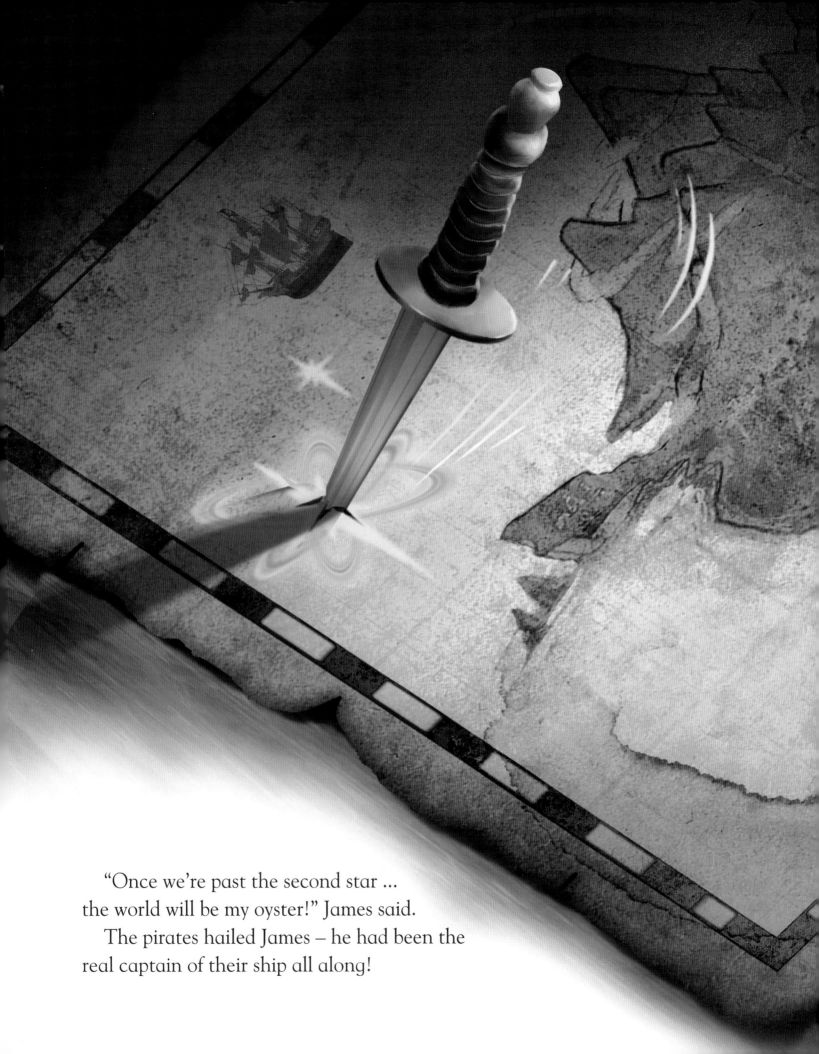

"Once we're past the second star ...
the world will be my oyster!" James said.
    The pirates hailed James – he had been the
real captain of their ship all along!

Down in the galley, Rosetta's crocodile had hopped through a cannon hole. The baby croc pulled down the crate holding the fairies. He wanted his favourite fairy friend!

The cook tried to catch his prisoners, but the croc
bit him and the fairies managed to get away.

The fairies sneaked off the ship and snatched the bottle of
Blue Dust from the Pixie Dust Tree.

"Return that Blue Dust!" James called to the fairies as they
flew across the deck. He dangled the lantern holding Zarina
above the water. "Or your friend is done for!"

The fairies didn't want Zarina to get hurt. Tink sadly flew
back to the tree and replaced the Blue Dust. James grabbed the
bottle and then threw Zarina into the water anyway.

The fairies rushed to rescue Zarina. They managed
to pull the lantern to the surface, but Zarina was still in
trouble because water was pouring into the lamp!

The fairies struggled with the latch. Finally,
it opened just in time and Zarina was saved!

Zarina was
grateful to Tink
and her friends.
She apologized and
offered to help them
catch James.

Zarina led the fairies to
the flying ship, but the second
star was not far away. They slipped
into the captain's cabin undetected – and
reappeared looking like swashbucklers! The real pirates
couldn't believe their eyes.

"Get them off my ship!" James commanded.

The pirates laughed at the fairies' tiny weapons.
It was quickly clear to the girls that they could not
defeat the pirates with their weapons – they needed
to use their new talents!

Fawn blasted a pirate named Bonito with a sunbeam,
knocking him overboard. Meanwhile, Rosetta went after
the cook on her crocodile. While trying to escape,
the cook threw his favourite clock,
which the baby crocodile
swallowed in one gulp!

As Zarina fought James, she managed to trap him using the mast and snatch the Blue Dust from him.

Zarina spun the wheel of the ship and it began to tilt. James's precious golden dust streamed off the ship and when James reached for it, he fell.

As Zarina helped the other fairies, James, now covered in golden dust, flew up behind her and claimed the Blue Dust back.

But he dropped one speck. Zarina quickly grabbed it and threw it on James who then rocketed into the air, out of control.

"From a trickle to a roar," she said with satisfaction.

Then, Tink used her water talent to create a giant wave in James's path, washing off all the golden dust. He crashed into the sea, where the baby crocodile swam after him.

The fairies had won! They took control of the ship and
flew it back to Pixie Hollow. When they reached
the amphitheatre, Zarina used her dust to wake the
sleeping crowd.

"Zarina?" Fairy Gary exclaimed. "You're home!" And he
pulled her into a giant hug.

"She even grew a Pixie Dust Tree!" exclaimed Rosetta.
Now, they had two.

Queen Clarion was so impressed that she granted Zarina permission to show off her new talent.

Colours flew as Zarina gave her friends back their original talents and the crowd was in awe!